Mozzarella and Murder

Book Thirteen

in

Papa Pacelli's

Pizzeria Series

By

Patti Benning

Copyright 2017 Summer Prescott Books

Author's Note: On the next page, you'll find out how to access all of my books easily, as well as locate books by best-selling author, Summer Prescott. I'd love to hear your thoughts on my books, the storylines, and anything else that you'd like to comment on – reader feedback is very important to me. Please see the following page for my publisher's contact information. If you'd like to be on her list of "folks to contact" with updates, release and sales notifications, etc…just shoot her an email and let her know. Thanks for reading!

Also…

…if you're looking for more great reads, from me and Summer, check out the Summer Prescott Publishing Book Catalog:

http://summerprescottbooks.com/book-catalog/ for some truly delicious stories.

Contact Info for Summer Prescott Publishing:

Twitter: @summerprescott1

Blog and Book Catalog: http://summerprescottbooks.com

Email: summer.prescott.cozies@gmail.com

And...look up The Summer Prescott Fan Page and Summer Prescott Publishing Page on Facebook – let's be friends!

To sign up for our fun and exciting newsletter, which will give you opportunities to win prizes and swag, enter contests, and be the first to know about New Releases, click   here: https://forms.aweber.com/form/02/1682036602.htm

TABLE OF CONTENTS

CHAPTER ONE... 10

CHAPTER TWO.. 20

CHAPTER THREE 26

CHAPTER FOUR 33

CHAPTER FIVE 41

CHAPTER SIX 51

CHAPTER SEVEN 60

CHAPTER EIGHT... 69

CHAPTER NINE 79

CHAPTER TEN 86

CHAPTER ELEVEN 94

CHAPTER TWELVE 100

CHAPTER THIRTEEN 108

CHAPTER FOURTEEN 114

CHAPTER FIFTEEN... 125

MOZZARELLA AND
MURDER

Book Thirteen In Papa Pacelli's Pizzeria Series

CHAPTER ONE

"She still isn't answering." Eleanora Pacelli passed the phone to her grandmother. "Can you hand me this if she calls back? I want to pick up the animals on the way home, but I don't want to just show up if she isn't expecting us."

"Do you think something happened?" Nonna asked. "It's been a while since we've heard from her. I hope the animals are okay."

"Me too."

Ellie gripped the steering wheel, trying to ignore the anxiety that was gnawing at her. She hadn't heard from their pet sitter for nearly three days. She hadn't been worried at first—cellphone service could be spotty all the way in the middle of nowhere on the northern coast of

Maine, and she knew a storm had recently blown through the area. It wasn't until today, when they were boarding the plane that would bring them home from Florida, that she had begun to get nervous.

Now that they were on their way home from the airport in Portland, she began to wonder if something was seriously wrong. Had something happened to the sitter… or to their pets? They would be arriving in Kittiport in just over an hour, and the original plan had been to stop on their way home to pick up the animals, her little black and white papillon, Bunny, and her grandfather's greenwing macaw, Marlowe. It wouldn't be the same at home without them, and besides, she would have to pay for another night of pet setting if she waited to pick them up until tomorrow. They had originally planned the pickup today with the pet sitter, but she wasn't sure what she should do now that the woman wasn't answering. Would it be rude to just drop by anyway?

"It's ringing," Nonna said, handing her back her phone. Keeping her eyes on the road, Ellie answered it with one hand and pressed it to her ear. "Hello?"

"Hey, Ellie," a familiar voice said.

"Hey, Russ." It was the first time that Ellie had ever been disappointed to hear the sheriff's voice. If only Samantha would call her back, then she could quit worrying and simply enjoy being home.

"I just wanted to make sure that you and your grandmother got off the plane safely. Did the flight go smoothly?"

"Everything went just fine," Ellie said. "It was sad to leave Florida, but I'm glad to be back. It will be wonderful to get home."

"Have you heard from the pet sitter yet? Do you think you'll be able to get the animals before going to the house?"

"Not yet. I don't know what I should do. Do you think it would be rude to stop by without talking to her first?"

"No, not if you had planned to stop there after your flight and she knows that you're going to be there. You know how spotty service can be up here, she's probably expecting you, but just can't get through. Do you want me to meet you there just in case?"

Ellie frowned. If Russell was offering to meet them there, that meant that he thought that there was a chance that something was seriously wrong. The thought wasn't comforting.

"No," she said at last. "I think we'll be fine. She probably just hasn't been able to get through, like you said. Thanks for the offer, though. I'll let you know everything's fine once we have the animals."

"Okay. I'm sure she'll be waiting at the door for you. Do you want me to come by tonight? I can bring dinner for the three of us if you want—pizza?"

"That would be wonderful," she replied.

She hung up, slightly mollified at the thought that she would be seeing Russell that night. It had only been a week since she had last seen him, but it felt like it had been ages. She would see Russell tonight, then tomorrow she would go in to Papa Pacelli's, the pizzeria that her grandfather had opened twenty years ago. She was eager to see how her employees had gotten along without her. According to them, everything had gone smoothly, but she wouldn't fully believe that until she saw it with her own eyes.

"Russell thinks that we should just stop by the pet sitter's house even if we don't hear from her," she said to her grandmother. "So, I guess that's what we're going to do. I'm sure everything is fine. In just a couple of hours, all four of us will be relaxing at home."

"I'm sure you're right, dear," Nonna said. She fell silent and looked out the window for a few minutes before speaking again. "You know, it's nice to be home."

"Yes, it is," Ellie said. It did feel good to have the familiar landscape around her. Even the air smelled different than it had in Florida. She hadn't realized just how homesick she had been until she had stepped out of the Portland airport.

She knew that her grandmother was still considering renting a condo part time in Florida, but the key word was part time. She was glad that Nonna would always be coming home to Maine. No matter how much she'd liked her vacation, she didn't think that she wanted to move anytime soon, and she couldn't imagine that her grandmother would want to leave her hometown permanently, either. Kittiport was the place where they would both always return.

They pulled into Samantha's driveway nearly an hour later, both of them tired and very ready to be on their way home. Ellie heard a familiar yapping coming from inside, and felt a rush of relief. Bunny, at least, was okay. She would recognize her dog's bark anywhere.

Nonna waited in the car while she got out and walked up the front porch to knock on the door. She waited for a moment, then knocked again. There was no answer, except for Bunny's yapping and, a moment later, a loud screech. *It sounds like Marlowe is fine, too,* she thought. *But where is Samantha?* There was a car in the driveway, but no sign of anyone being in the house. Frowning, Ellie knocked for a third time, pounding on the door much harder than she had before. Still, nothing.

"Samantha?" she called "Are you there?"

There was no reply. Ellie hesitated for only a second, before reaching for the doorknob. Her dog was inside; she couldn't just walk away.

The doorknob turned, but the door itself seemed to be stuck on something. Ellie put her shoulder to it and pushed, and managed to open it just enough for a little black and white ball of fur to slip through the crack.

"Bunny!" she exclaimed, lunging for the dog, terrified that she would run into the road. Luckily, the papillon seemed too excited to see her to consider running away. She was bouncing around Ellie's legs, her little tail wagging so fast it was a blur. She knelt down and scooped the dog up. Bunny squirmed in her arms, licking her frantically. She smelled terrible, her nose was dry, and she felt much lighter than she had when Ellie had dropped her off. She knew immediately that something was seriously wrong.

"What happened to you?" she asked.

She hurried back down to the car and handed Bunny to her grandmother through the passenger side window. "Here, you take her. I need to go and see what's going on."

16

She returned to the front porch and eventually managed to get the door shoved open enough for her to go inside. She slipped through, then nearly tripped over her own feet as she realized what she had just stepped over.

"Oh, my goodness," she said, pressing her hands to her mouth. The pet sitter's body was slouched against the front door. There was a dark smear on the doorknob, and another dark smudge partway down the door. She wasn't any sort of expert, but she thought that the body had been there for a few days at least. The house smelled terrible, and she tried not to gag as she stumbled even further back from the body.

"Hi!"

The word had come from only feet away. Ellie screamed and whirled around to come face to face with a red parrot in a big cage. It took her a moment to catch her breath and slow her pounding heart down enough that she could speak.

"Hi, Marlowe," she managed. "You nearly gave me a heart attack."

She noticed the empty food dish and the slimy water bowl in the bird's cage, along with the smattering of bare spots across the bird's chest where she had plucked out her own feathers. The sight made her heart ache, and she knew that she had gotten there just in time for the animals, even if she hadn't made it in time to save the pet sitter.

CHAPTER TWO

Ellie knew that she should leave the house. Every second she stayed, she was disturbing evidence. However, the thought of leaving Marlowe was hard. Even harder was the knowledge that to leave the home, she would have to step around the dead body again, at least if she wanted to go through the front door.

The gate out back has a lock on it, she thought, remembering her tour from the week before. The pet sitter had a tall fence with padlocked gates to prevent someone from leaving the gate open accidentally—or worse, from stealing one of the dogs while they were outside. That concession to safety had been one of the reasons that Ellie had chosen this pet sitter. That, and the fact that Samantha worked at the local veterinary clinic. If anything went wrong, Ellie had thought that she would be able to handle it. *Except for this,* she thought, unable to tear her gaze away from the dead woman. She was going to have to go past her again. It was the only way out.

Bracing herself, Ellie stepped carefully around the woman's body, trying not to look too much at the dark smudges of blood on the door. She slipped outside, ignoring the macaw's loud screech behind her. She hated leaving Marlowe alone in there, but she knew that right now the most important thing was for her to call the police.

Her grandmother rolled down the passenger side window as she approached, keeping a tight grip on the dog in her lap. "What happened?" she asked. "This little dog is skin and bones. Ellie, what's going on?"

"The pet sitter… she's dead," Ellie said, hardly believing it even as she said it.

Her grandmother was shocked into silence. She tightened her grip on Bunny, and rummaged around with her other hand until she found Ellie's cellphone, which she handed to her. Ellie's fingers were shaking as she dialed the familiar number.

"Hey, did you get the thing with the pet sitter sorted out?" he asked when he answered the call.

"Russell, you have to get down here right away. I went inside, I didn't know I would find her dead. Her body is right in front of the door. It's so horrible. We have Bunny in the car, but Marlowe is still inside. I don't know what to do. Please, hurry." She knew that she was speaking too quickly, but couldn't seem to stop her tongue from tripping over itself.

"I'll grab Liam and we'll head right over," he said, grasping the situation despite her frantic words. "Don't touch anything else. Are you sure that she's dead?"

Ellie wondered if he was trying to decide whether to call an ambulance or the coroner. "Yes. She is. She's... she's been there for a few days."

"Ah. Okay. We'll hurry. You two just sit tight. Ellie... It'll be okay."

He hung up. She slid the phone into her pocket and walked around to the driver's door, still feeling stunned. She pulled the door open and sat down in the car. After a moment, Bunny wriggled away from her grandmother and climbed into her lap. She patted the dog, feeling her heart ache, both for the animals that had been forced to go for days without any care, and for the pet sitter. Poor Marlowe was still inside. She hoped that the bird wasn't too traumatized. The poor thing had witnessed both her grandfather's death, and now this young woman's passing. It must have left an impact, especially on an animal as intelligent as the parrot was.

While they waited, Ellie let Bunny lap up some water from her water bottle. She was glad that they had stopped by when they did. If they had decided to go home and wait for the pet sitter to get back to them, there was no telling what would have happened to the animals. What had happened to the poor woman? She remembered the smudge of blood on the doorknob. That must have been where she had hit her head, but how had she fallen? She must have tripped over something.

Ellie looked down at the little dog in her lap. What if Samantha had tripped over Bunny, and that had been what killed her? The thought made her feel ill, and she pushed it away. She wanted Russell to get there and tell her it would all be okay. He was the one that knew how to deal with situations like this, not her.

She heard the sirens before she saw the flashing lights come around the corner. It was wonderful to see the familiar sheriff's truck approaching them, thought it wasn't quite how she had imagined their reunion would be.

Russell pulled into the driveway, closely followed by his deputy, Liam, in another cruiser. Ellie handed Bunny back to her grandmother and rushed forward to meet him. The sheriff pulled her into a strong hug, and she felt herself relax, just slightly. Despite everything, it was wonderful to see him again. With another mysterious death, it looked like her return to Kittiport promised to be anything but boring.

CHAPTER THREE

The sheriff pulled back after a moment and looked her up and down. "Are you okay?" he asked.

"I'm fine," she said. "But that poor woman, Russell. How could something like this have happened?"

"That's what I'm going to find out," he said firmly. "Do you have keys to the place?"

"No. When she didn't answer, I tried the door. It was unlocked. She's… she's just inside."

He nodded, turned to Liam, and began giving orders. The coroner's van pulled up alongside the curb while he was speaking and the men inside unloaded a gurney. Ellie, however, had eyes only for Russell. He was dressed more nicely than usual—a dark blue button-down shirt, black slacks, shiny black loafers. She wondered what sort of event he had come from. She was out of the loop from having been gone for an entire week, and she had ħo idea where he might have been.

She waited outside while he and Liam investigated the house. She heard Marlowe screech when they went in, then heard the bird's cheerful "Hi!" when she realized that she knew one of the men walking through the door. Ellie's heart began to ache again for the poor animals. They must have been so frightened and confused.

After Liam had thoroughly documented the scene with photos, the coroners' technicians took the body away. Ellie looked away when they pushed the gurney outside. While the van pulled away, Russell came and stood next Ellie. "I have just a few questions," he said. "Do you want to do this now, or do you need to get home? I could come over in a little while if you need some time."

"If it won't take long, let's just do it now," Ellie said. "Do you have any idea what happened to her?"

"Just from this first look at the scene, it appears that she tripped and fell over something and hit her head quite hard on the doorknob. The body will be going in for an autopsy, which should tell us if there's anything else at play here. I did find two glasses inside on the counter, but even if she had a guest over the day that she died, that doesn't mean that he or she had anything to do with her death."

"So, you do think it was an accident?" Ellie asked.

"It appears that way, but I can't say for sure yet. How well did you know her?"

"Not very well. I saw her flyer at the pet store and took her number since I was looking for a pet sitter for the week that we were in Florida. I met her once before dropping the animals off. I called her references and she checked out, and she worked at the vet's office. She seemed like such a nice, respectful young lady. When she stopped answering my texts, I thought that something might be wrong, but I never imagined this."

"How did she act when you dropped off the animals? Did she seem distracted, worried, or frightened at all?

Anything to indicate that she might be in some sort of trouble?"

"No, she seemed just fine," Ellie said. "And she never mentioned anything during the texts and emails we exchanged while I was in Florida. Everything seemed to be going perfectly."

"Depending on what the investigation turns up, I might want to go through your communications with her." He sighed. "Sorry, Ellie, I know that this isn't how you wanted things to be when you came back. I'll let you get going now, but first I'll go in with you so you can grab Marlowe."

"Thanks," she said, falling into step next to him. "So, what's with the clothes? Were you in the middle of something important when I called?"

"Oh…" He looked down at himself, as if he had forgotten what he was wearing. "No, I just happened to throw this on this morning. Don't worry about me—I'm just glad that you're okay. It must have been terrible finding her like that."

"It was."

Ellie looked toward the house and shivered. She wasn't eager to go back inside to get Marlowe, but she knew that she couldn't ask Russell to do it. The bird would be scared enough as it was, and she probably wouldn't handle Russell trying to grab her very well. She hoped that Samantha had kept the bird's carrier somewhere easy to reach. There was no question of leaving Marlowe at the house overnight, so if she couldn't find the carrier, she would just have to improvise.

Liam was still inside the house, sifting through Samantha's possessions, looking for any evidence of foul play in her death. He nodded at her when she came inside, and she gave him a quick wave. She liked both of Russell's deputies. They were good people, and she would trust either of them with her life.

She approached the bird's cage, looking around for the smaller pet carrier. "How am I going to bring you home?" she asked the bird. "Where did Samantha put your carrier?"

Liam made a noise behind her, and when she turned, he pointed toward the opposite corner. "There's a pet carrier over there, between the couch and the wall, if that's what you're looking for."

"Thanks," she said.

She found the carrier and carried it over to the birdcage. When she opened the cage door, Marlowe eagerly stepped onto her arm. "Into the carrier you go," she told the bird. "We'll go home, and you'll get as much fresh water and food as you want. And maybe even some cookies if I can find any."

Marlowe went into the pet carrier without complaint. Ellie shut and locked it, then carried it out to the car, putting it in the backseat. She had her family back together at last. It wasn't exactly the homecoming that she had envisioned, but she knew that she had a lot to be thankful for. If they had stayed in Florida for just a couple more days, the animals might not have made it.

CHAPTER FOUR

Fifteen minutes later, Ellie pulled into the familiar driveway. The old white house stood on a lonely stretch of the coastal highway. The property was bordered on the back by a state forest; in the front, across the road and down a shallow hill, was the ocean. The neighbors' houses were far enough away that it was often easy to forget that there were other people around. In the front yard stood a towering white pine, which Ellie had decorated for Christmas the year before. There was a detached garage next to the house, which housed her grandfather's ancient truck. A stone path led to the front stoop, and around back was a flagstone patio.

Ellie pulled up as far as she could before shutting off the engine, knowing that her back would thank her later, once she got done unloading the luggage. Bunny, who was sitting on her grandmother's lap, was vibrating with excitement. Ellie thought that in this situation, the animals might be even more glad to get home than she was. After what had happened, she didn't blame them. Returning home was, for her and her grandmother, the end of the pleasant vacation. For the animals, it would be an escape from what had probably been three or four days of absolute horror. She forced herself to push the thought of the animals' suffering out of her mind. She could think about it later, for now she had to concentrate on getting everyone inside, setting up the parrot and the dog with food and water, and unpacking.

She left Marlowe in the car while she helped her grandmother out of the passenger seat and took Bunny into her own arms. She had been in such a hurry to get away from the pet sitter's house that she hadn't thought to look for the little dog's leash, but it wasn't much of a loss. A leash she could replace. She unlocked the front door and held it open for her grandmother. Then, she put Bunny down on the grass and waited while she sniffed around. The poor dog must have been forced to relieve herself in the house while she was trapped inside, something that she knew Bunny would hate. The thought made her more patient than usual while she waited for the dog to finish up with her business before going inside.

Ellie followed her grandmother into the kitchen, and grabbed Bunny's bowl off the floor, filling it to the brim with fresh, cold water before returning to the car to grab Marlowe. The bird seemed overjoyed to see her own familiar cage again. Ellie let her climb inside and settle herself on her favorite perch before she shut the cage door. Then she grabbed the bird's dishes from the side doors and filled one with water and the other with the bird's fruit-colored pellets. The macaw went straight for the food when Ellie slid the dish back into the cage. Ellie watched her for a moment, glad to see Marlowe eating so heartily. She was glad that both animals seemed mostly okay after the ordeal. She would have to schedule them both vet appointments just to set her own mind at ease, but by the looks of things, both would recover just fine.

She returned to the kitchen where Bunny was still lapping up the water in her own bowl. Nonna was at the counter, preparing the dog's food. Ellie had to smile when she saw how full the bowl was. She didn't know if the little papillon's stomach was that big. Her grandmother had mixed together kibble, canned dog food, tuna, and by the looks of it, a little bit of shredded cheese from the fridge.

"You know, I think she would've been perfectly happy with just some kibble," Ellie said.

"After what she's been through, she deserves this," her grandmother said. "I'll take care of her. Can you bring in the luggage? I'm getting tired, and I want to sit down for a bit, but I want to start unpacking first."

"Sure, I'll go and grab it. Thanks for getting her food. Just don't let her eat so much that she gets sick. I'm going to call the vet when they get back in and set up appointments for both of them, just to make sure they're okay."

She went outside and began unloading the car. It was a bit bittersweet as she carried in their bags. She had really enjoyed the trip to Florida, or at least she'd enjoyed the last half of it. It had been wonderful to spend some extra time with her grandmother, and to take some time to relax and enjoy the beautiful, sub-tropical beaches on her own.

She had made a wonderful new friend while she was down there, and had embarked on a brand-new business opportunity. It had been less than a day since they had flown out of Miami, but after everything that had happened in the past few hours, the vacation seemed like a lifetime ago.

She brought her grandmother's bags into the older woman's bedroom on the lower floor, and then dragged her own up the stairs. She tossed her suitcase onto the bed, then sat down next to it. It felt good to be home. She really had missed everything and everyone here.

I wonder why Russell was so dressed up, she mused as she leaned back against the pillows, enjoying the cool, air-conditioned room and the soft mattress. She didn't know why he would lie to her, but she also didn't think that he had just accidentally put on such nice clothes. Maybe he would tell her later. She hoped that he wouldn't be too busy with this new case, and that it got resolved quickly. She felt terrible for Samantha. It was always especially hard for her when a younger person died. The young woman's entire future had been stolen. It was heartbreaking. If Ellie wasn't also so worried about the animals, she would've been even more focused on Samantha's death. In a way, she was glad for the distraction. The animals she could care for. There was nothing she could do for the young pet sitter. As it was, she couldn't help thinking about everything that she and the woman said to each other. Had Samantha been in trouble, and she had just failed to notice?

She got up and unzipped her carry-on to pull her laptop out. She propped it up on her suitcase and sat cross-legged in front of it, waiting for the screen to load. Once the computer was awake, she clicked into her email account, where she began going through the exchanges between her and Samantha. She was looking for anything even slightly unusual, something that might give a hint as some sort of trouble the young woman might have been in.

A few minutes later, she closed the computer. She had found nothing. Her exchanges with Samantha had all been about Bunny and Marlowe, and the pet sitter had been positive and upbeat the entire time. If something darker had been going on in her life, she had done a very good job of keeping it from Ellie.

CHAPTER FIVE

The next day, Ellie left the house early, eager to get to the pizzeria and have some time to settle in before the restaurant opened. It felt wonderful to walk in through the employee entrance and find herself and the familiar clean kitchen. Her employees had done well while she was gone. Everything had been wiped down, no dishes were left over from the day before, and the dining area was spic and span. Even the soda fridge was fully stocked.

She walked around the little restaurant slowly, appreciating the wonderful feeling of homecoming. There, on the wall behind the register, was the twentieth anniversary picture of her grandmother standing in front of the restaurant. Beside it was a picture back when the restaurant had first opened. She hoped that in another twenty years, a third picture might join them. She loved this restaurant, every bit as much as her grandfather had. She was excited at the thought of opening the second Papa Pacelli's down in Florida, but this one would always have a special place in her heart.

Once she had finished with her walkthrough, she returned to the kitchen to begin making the first pizza of the day. This would be lunch—and probably also dinner—for herself. The wonderful thing about being able to make her own pizzas like this was that she could put absolutely anything that she wanted on them. Sometimes she experimented with odd ingredients, but today she thought that she would stick to the basics with a veggie supreme pizza. Their largest size would last her all day, with leftovers for her to take home for them to eat tomorrow.

After she had the dough rolled out, she put the crust in the oven to begin cooking while she prepared a variety of vegetables to top it. Her employees had kept the fridge well stocked, so she had no lack of ingredients to choose from. She chopped up red peppers and mushrooms, diced some fresh tomatoes, and sliced up half an onion. By the time she was done, the crust had finished precooking. She took it out of the oven, slathered some of their secret sauce on it, sprinkled a couple of generous handfuls of cheese over the sauce, and then added the vegetables. She put it back in the oven to finish cooking and begin cleaning up the mess she had made while she waited.

Ten minutes later, she was sitting at the little table in the corner of the kitchen, enjoying the best slice of pizza that she'd had in a week. She knew that she was biased, but she had found that nothing could really compare to pizza made from her grandfather's recipe. She was a little bit nervous about giving that recipe away to another woman, but she knew that Linda, the woman she had chosen to run the second Papa Pacelli's Pizzeria, was trustworthy. This, she thought, would be the first step in the restaurant's journey to more widespread fame. They were already locally famous, and she couldn't wait to see how the restaurant would do in another state.

She was just finishing up her second slice of pizza when she heard a key in the employee door. A moment later, Rose walked in. The young woman with beautiful blonde hair had been at the pizzeria for longer than Ellie had been. When Ellie had first met her, her first impression had been of a flighty girl who wouldn't be very reliable. Rose had quickly proven her wrong.

"Hey, Ms. P," Rose said. "I saw your car in the parking lot. I don't know if you've had a chance to look at the schedule yet, but Jacob and I are scheduled to work for today, with Pete on call if it gets busy. We didn't know if you would want to come in on your first day back from Florida. How was your vacation, anyway?"

"Well, other than one pretty major incident, it was wonderful. I'll tell everyone about it later," she said quickly, noticing the questioning expression on her employees' face. "It was a really nice break from normal life, but I'm glad to be back. I'm sure Jacob told you the news about the second store?"

"Yeah, he told all of us. He's pretty excited. Do you think it will change anything for us up here?" Rose asked.

"I don't see why it should," Ellie said. "The woman I found down there should be able to run it herself pretty well. I'll technically be her boss, but I shouldn't have to do much once the store is up and running. I'll probably fly down there in a few months to see how things are going. It will take a while for renovations to be done, anyway. I think we're planning on having the grand opening sometime in October."

"Neat. It would be cool if we could all go," the young woman said. "I'd love to see the other store sometime."

"Hey, that's a great idea," Ellie said. "Maybe we could all visit for the grand opening. It would mean closing down this store for a few days, though. I'll have to think about it."

She began packing up the rest of the pizza to put in the fridge while Rose went to the front and clocked in. It wasn't until she returned to the kitchen and began washing her hands that Ellie noticed how puffy and red her eyes were, as if she had been crying.

"Rose, is everything okay?" she asked.

She nodded. "I'm okay. I just got some news this morning about a friend of mine. She was found dead in her home yesterday. She was my age, and we went to school together. It's not something you ever expect to hear."

Ellie felt her stomach twist. "Was her name Samantha?"

"It was. How did you know?" the girl asked.

"I'm the one that found her," Ellie said. "She was pet sitting for me, and I stopped by the house yesterday to pick up the animals. That's when I discovered her."

"Oh, my goodness, I didn't know it was you," Rose said. "The paper just said that she had been found, it didn't say by who."

Ellie suspected the discretion was probably the work of Shannon Ward: her best friend, Russell's sister-in-law, and one of the journalists at the local newspaper. Shannon would have known that Ellie wouldn't want her name connected to yet another crime. She made a mental note to thank her friend when they got together sometime in the next couple of days.

"I'm so sorry," she told her employee. "She seemed like such a kind girl."

"She was. She loved animals. Did they say... how it happened?"

"The sheriff thinks this was an accident. It looks like she tripped and fell over something, and hit her head," Ellie said.

Rose nodded, looking slightly relieved. "When I first heard, I had to wonder if it was suicide. She was devastated when she lost her job at the vet clinic last week, and she and her boyfriend had split up shortly before that, so I knew that she was having a tough time."

"I didn't know she had lost her job. Do you know what happened?"

"No, just that she got fired. I was going to meet her last Saturday to talk more about it, but she never got back to me. Now I know why."

"You said that she and her boyfriend broke up? Do you know if it was a messy breakup?"

"I think they were still on pretty good terms." Rose frowned. "Why? I thought you said that it was an accident."

"They're still investigating. I wouldn't want them to miss anything important, that's all."

The young woman nodded. "Can I have the day of her funeral off? I'm not sure when it is yet, but I don't want to risk missing it."

"Of course," Ellie said. "I'll cover you if I have to. And if you want to take today off too—"

"No, no. I'm happy to be here. It helps take my mind off it. Plus, it gives me an excuse to keep my phone off. I know all of our friends are going to be wanting to talk about it, and I'd rather not, just now."

"If you're sure," Ellie said. "Just let me know if you need some time to yourself, and I'll make sure you get it."

Ellie watched her employee carefully for the next few hours as they settled into the workday. She was worried about Rose, but the young woman seemed to be holding up well. She thought once again just how horrible it was when a young person passed away before their time. If someone had been involved in Samantha's death, she hoped that Russell found them as quickly as possible. No one had the right to take someone's future away from them, no matter the reason.

CHAPTER SIX

The new green dress that she had bought in Florida suited her well. She turned around, looking over her shoulder in the mirror to make sure that she had removed all the tags. She had managed to get a bit of a tan on her vacation, and the shade of the dress helped to show it off. Her black hair was up in a ponytail—it was either that, or down, since she had never managed to convince it to take any other style. She had a pair of gold earrings that she had borrowed from her grandmother, and was wearing an old pair of black heels that she had borrowed from her mother years ago and never returned. The outfit came together well, and she was pleased.

This would be the first time that she had seen Russell since the day she had returned. It would be nice to simply spend time with him, without any dead bodies around. It had been far too long since they had gone on a date like this, and she was looking forward to it.

Bunny, who was doing much better after a few days of plentiful food and water, along with a bath and lots of brushing, was laying on the bed and watching her. The little dog had been especially clingy since her return from the pet sitter's. Ellie had been babying the papillon, maybe more than she should have been, but she couldn't help it. She still felt terrible about what her pets had gone through.

"Do you want to go outside before I leave?" Ellie asked. The dog's tail began to wag, but she didn't jump up with an eager bark like she used to when Ellie asked her that question.

She opened the bedroom door and waited for the little dog to jump off the bed. Bunny trailed her down the stairs, sticking close to her heels. When Marlowe saw them, she left her perch and climbed up the side of the cage, pressing her face against the bars. Ellie walked over and planted a kiss on the bird's beak.

"Nonna will take care of you both while I'm gone," she promised. "It will only be for a few hours."

She opened the back door and waited on the patio while Bunny sniffed at the lawn. She was glad that the dog had a vet appointment in a couple of days. It would put her mind at ease to know that there was nothing serious wrong with her. In time, she was sure, the papillon would be back to her normal, bouncy self.

After bringing the dog back inside, Ellie grabbed her purse and went to wait on the front stoop for Russell to arrive. It was an overcast evening, not yet raining, but the dark clouds were pregnant with the promise of it later that night. After the heat of Florida, the slightly cooler day felt nice to her. She enjoyed looking out over the ocean, grey and wavy though it was, and thought, not for the first time, just how lucky she was.

Russell pulled into the driveway few minutes later in his familiar, slightly beat-up sheriff's truck. She hurried over and slipped into the passenger seat before he could get out and open the door for her.

"Hey," she said as she kissed him on the cheek. "How are you?"

"I'm doing well. How are you? Are you glad to be back?"

"Yes, definitely. It was so nice to be back at the pizzeria yesterday. It's ridiculous how much I missed it. I know it's just a restaurant, but I love it. I was glad to see that the employees did such an excellent job taking care of everything. Even though I trust them, I couldn't help being worried about it."

"You have wonderful employees. I'm sure they would have told you if anything had gone wrong," he said as he back the truck into the road.

"I know. I need to learn to relax and trust them to do their jobs while I'm gone." She looked out the window at the trees, the tops of which were swaying in the wind. "It's sad, though," she said after a moment. "I found out yesterday that Rose knew Samantha. They were friends. It makes what happened seem even worse, somehow."

"I'm sorry for her," Russell said. "It's hard to lose a friend. Did she have anything to say about Samantha's death? Did she mention her friend being in any sort of trouble?"

"She seemed relieved when I told her how Samantha died. I guess she was worried that it might have been suicide. She told me that Samantha had lost her job at the vet clinic only a few days ago, and had also gone through a breakup not long before that."

"It sounds like the young woman had a lot on her plate. The autopsy will be done in a couple of days, and we'll know more then. I still think it looks like an accident on the surface, but there's something about it that just doesn't seem right to me."

"The poor girl," Ellie said. "I just can't get over how young she was."

"The young ones are always the hardest to deal with," Russell said. "This job definitely isn't getting any easier."

The rest of their drive to the restaurant was in silence. Ellie felt bad for bringing up the case. She didn't want that to be the focus of their evening. She wanted to have a nice date with her boyfriend, not dwell on a tragedy that neither of them could change.

Russell had reserved a table for them at the White Pine Kitchen, the nicest restaurant in town. They were seated within minutes of walking through the doors, and soon he and Ellie were perusing the menus. Everything looked good to her. It had been a busy few days, and she hadn't had a chance to sit down for a real meal since she had gotten back. She had been mostly subsisting on pizza and whatever baked goods her grandmother made during the day.

"I still have to thank Shannon. She's the one that kept my name out of the paper, isn't she?" she asked the sheriff, looking up from her menu.

"Yes, that was all her," Russell said. "She's a good friend… and a good sister-in-law."

"She really is. I'm hoping to have lunch with her this weekend. There's so much we have to catch up on. It's been almost two weeks since we've seen each other. I can't believe how much has changed. Everything that happened in Florida, the second pizzeria…"

"When do you think it will open? It's an exciting step for you."

"We're thinking sometime in October," Ellie said. "Rose had a great idea yesterday. I'm thinking of flying us all down there for the grand opening. It will be wonderful for the employees from both stores to get to know each other, and I'll feel better having more control over the grand opening. I want to make sure everything is perfect. What do you think? Would you be able to come?"

"If I can get the time off work, I'd love to. Let me know the dates as soon as possible."

"I will let you know as soon as I know," she promised. "It would be quite fun, wouldn't it? Maybe Shannon and James could come, too."

"I think it would be wonderful," Russell said. He smiled at her. "Congratulations on the second restaurant. I'm proud of you. I can't wait to see where all of this goes."

"Me either," Ellie said. "Florida might just be the first step. Who knows what could happen next?"

She smiled as she thought about all the possibilities. She had never imagined this future for herself, but now she wouldn't give it up for anything.

CHAPTER SEVEN

Her phone rang early the next morning. She fumbled around on her nightstand until she found it, then pulled it into bed. Bunny, sleeping on pillow beside her, stirred slightly. Ellie squinted at the caller ID. She was surprised to see that it was Russell. She slid her finger across the screen to accept the call, then pressed the cellphone to her ear.

"Hello?" she asked, groggily.

"Hey, Ellie," he said. "Sorry to wake you. I'm on my way to the sheriff's department now. The autopsy report came in early, and some of the notes are making me think that this wasn't an accident at all. I'm going to go over all the evidence again, and it would help if you could bring in your phone and computer so I can see the emails and text that she sent you. I'm also going to need your employee's contact information. She might know something that could be of help to this case."

"Okay," she said, sitting up and rubbing her eyes with her other hand. "I'll stop by in a couple of hours, if you can wait that long. I've got to drop my grandmother off at her aquatic therapy class this morning. I'll send you Rose's contact information as soon as I get off the phone."

"That's fine," Russell said. "I'll be here all day. There's got to be something I'm missing."

She hung up and looked toward the window. The curtains were drawn, but she could see the sunlight filtering in around the edges. She had never been a morning person, and today was no exception. She tried futilely for a few minutes to get back to sleep, but it was too late. Her mind kept being drawn back to thoughts of Samantha's death—or, if Russell was right, her murder. With a sigh, she got up and went downstairs, saying good morning to Marlowe on her way by as she took Bunny outside to do her business. The dog wasn't any more used to the early hours than she was, and trotted right into the living room to curl up on the couch when she was done.

An hour later, Ann Pacelli walked out of her bedroom to find a kitchen table set with bacon, fresh blueberry pancakes, eggs, and orange juice. Marlowe was on a wooden perch by the patio door, looking outside, and Ellie was scrubbing dishes at the sink.

"Look at this," Nonna said. "This is wonderful. What's the occasion?"

"I couldn't sleep," Ellie said told her. "I started cooking, and, well, this just sort of happened. Go ahead and sit down. We should start eating before it gets cold. We have your aquatic therapy session in an hour, and I have to stop at the sheriff's department afterward to see Russell about the pet sitter's case."

"After eating all of this, I might be too full to swim," her grandmother joked as she sat down. "Thanks again for driving me. I hope it isn't interrupting your day too much."

"Not at all. You know I don't mind. After everything you've done for me, what's a ride into town?"

They ate breakfast together in a companionable silence, interrupted only by the occasional soft sound from

Marlowe reacting to the wild birds on the other side of the window, and the jingle of Bunny's tags at she sniffed around under the table looking for dropped crumbs. It was a peaceful morning, with only thoughts of Samantha intruding to distract her. She hoped that this case was solved quickly. She was only beginning to realize the impact that Russell's job must have on him. He saw death more often than most people, and it couldn't be easy for him.

After breakfast, Ellie and her grandmother went their separate ways to get ready for the day. They met back up at the front door just in the nick of time. Any later, and they would be late for the session at the community pool. Ellie had her hand on the doorknob and was about to pull the door closed when she heard from inside something that made her jump.

"Stop it!"

The words had been shouted in a woman's voice. The phrase was repeated a moment later, this time followed by a loud squawk. She realized that it was Marlowe, and released a breath that she hadn't known she had been holding. That was new.

"Where did she pick that up?" Nonna wondered as Ellie shut and locked the door.

"I have no idea," Ellie said. "Maybe it's something she heard at the pet sitter's house." She felt her skin crawl. Was she hearing the murdered woman's last words? She shivered. This was definitely something she would share with Russell when she saw him.

An hour later, she was standing in line at the local coffee shop just a few doors down from the sheriff's department. She had ordered her and Russell's favorite drinks, thinking that they might both need a boost of caffeine to get through the day ahead of them.

Mrs. Lafferre, the secretary, greeted her with a smile when she came in. "It's nice you back in town, Eleanora," she said.

"It's good to be back," Ellie replied. She stopped by the front desk and dropped off a croissant for the older woman.

Mrs. Lafferre, Liam's grandmother, was the only person who called Ellie by her full name. She had taken over as a temporary secretary when the previous woman had left for maternity leave, but by the looks of things, she was going to stay. She could be a little bit forgetful, but Ellie found herself liking the tough old woman.

After dropping off the croissant, Ellie let herself through the door to the back of the sheriff's department and made her way to Russell's office, where she knocked on the doorframe before peeking into the open door. He waved for her to come the rest of the way in.

"Here, this is for you," she said handing over the coffee.

"Thanks," he said. "I gave your employee a call. She'll be coming in this evening. Do you have the laptop?"

"Yep. Here you go. And here's my phone. Do whatever you need to transfer the emails and texts over."

"Thanks."

"So, what did the coroner's report say?" she asked, taking the seat across from him.

There were some unexplained bruises on her body, bruises that she wouldn't have gotten from falling. She also had alcohol in her system, and some still in her stomach. She was drinking right before she died, and she wasn't drinking alone."

"So, that means that she was probably killed by someone that she knew," Ellie guessed. "I doubt she would let a complete stranger into her house and drink with them."

"Sadly, you're probably right. There are a few people that we're going to talk to today, and her ex-boyfriend is at the top of that list. Hopefully her friend, Rose, will be able to help point us in the right direction. I'm also going to be calling the vet's office to find out why she was let go. If she made a mistake that caused the death of someone's pet, that could be our motive right there."

"She worked at the clinic right here in town, right?" Ellie asked.

"Yes. The vet that she worked under is Dr. George Morgan," Russell said.

"That's Bunny's vet. We're going to see him tomorrow. I think he knows my grandmother—they're about the same age."

"I don't want you to go out of your way to do any investigating while you're there, but if you hear anything suspicious, definitely let me know."

"I will," Ellie said. "It sounds like you're going to be pretty busy. I'll get out of your hair as soon as you're done getting what you need from my phone and computer."

"You can stay for a while, if you'd like," he said. "It's nice to have you back in town. I missed you while you were gone."

"I've got to pick up my grandmother in about half an hour," Ellie said. "I'll stay until then."

"Good." He leaned across the table to give her a quick kiss before returning his attention to the computers.

CHAPTER EIGHT

Ellie parked outside the community pool and waited for her grandmother. A few minutes past eleven, she saw the doors open and a group of elderly men and women came out. The instructor wasn't with them, which was unusual. Ellie had met the man a couple of times, and he usually came out to make sure everyone who didn't drive had rides to get home.

She watched as Nonna said goodbye to her friends and began to make her way slowly across the grass. As she neared, Ellie leaned over and opened door for her. Nonna sat down in the passenger seat, setting her purse on her lap. Her hair was still wet, and she smelled like chlorine.

"Did everything go well?" Ellie asked. "I know you missed last week's lesson."

"I probably spent more time in the water last week than they did," her grandmother said. "The lesson was fine. I got to tell everyone about our Florida trip, which was nice. And when I told them about what Marlowe said this morning, they got shivers."

"It was creepy," Ellie agreed. "Where's the instructor? Usually he comes out to make sure everyone has a ride home."

"He left early. One of the other nice young people took over for him. It was a small class today; George left early as well, and then Catherine got a cramp and had to sit out for a while. You know," Nonna lowered her voice, "I think I'm doing better than a lot of these people."

"Well, that's good," Ellie said, pulling away from the curb. "You've got to be active to stay healthy, and you certainly keep active enough for three of you."

"Active and hungry," Nonna said. "Do you want to stop for lunch on the way home? Swimming always makes me feel as if I'm starving afterward."

"Sure. Do you want to try that little deli on the corner? They had pretty good soup last time we were in. I'm not really in the mood for pizza, I've been eating way too much of it since we got back."

"I'm okay with wherever you take me to," her grandmother said, settling back in her seat. "This is nice. It's just like having a chauffeur."

Ellie drove them to deli, where they sat at a small bistro table by the window. Ellie ordered soup, and her grandmother got a sandwich and salad. After a little while, Nonna cleared her throat and looked up from her food.

"Just so you know, I have a date tomorrow evening. He'll be picking me up at the house."

"That's wonderful," Ellie exclaimed. "Who is it with?"

"George. He asked me right before he left. Isn't that nice?"

Ellie wasn't sure who George was—her grandmother had so many friends, she could never keep their names straight. Still, it was wonderful that her grandmother was opening herself up to the possibility of a new relationship.

"I think it's going to be great for you," she said. "Just let me know if you need any help getting ready."

After that, she told her grandmother about the plan that she was beginning to form to fly back to Florida in October. "Of course, you don't have to come with us if you aren't up to it. I'm just thinking how nice it would be for everyone to go together. I want the people working at the new pizzeria to feel like family too."

"I would love to come," Nonna said. "If we go as late as October, well… I might stay there for a few months on my own after the grand opening."

Ellie put down her spoon, surprised. She knew that her grandmother had been thinking about renting or leasing one of the condos in the retirement community where her friends were, but she hadn't known that her grandmother was thinking about it for this coming year. It would be odd to be in the big house alone over winter, but she thought that it would probably be better, certainly safer, for her grandmother to be somewhere warm and pleasant, somewhere without three feet of snow on the ground.

"Okay. I think it would be wonderful for you. I'd miss having you here, of course. How long do you think you'd stay for?"

"I'm not sure yet. I haven't really made up my mind. Are you sure you would you be okay all alone here, though? I won't go if you don't want me to."

"I'm sure I would manage," Ellie said. "I have Shannon and Russell, and the animals. And the pizzeria, of course. Maybe I could fly down around Christmastime and visit you if you stay that long."

"That would be wonderful," Nonna said. She smiled. "I'm so excited for all of this. Before we left, I was beginning to feel as if my life wasn't going anywhere. I thought I would just keep doing the same things day after day until I died. I know it's a little bit dark, but it's the truth. Now, I feel like there's so many possibilities ahead of me. Thank you. I think the trip was really good for me."

"I'm glad," Ellie said. "I enjoyed it as well. I'm glad I got the chance to go with you. Even with everything that happened. I don't think I'll ever forget our trip."

After their pleasant lunch, the two of them got back in the car and Ellie drove toward the Pacelli house. She took her time as they wound down the coastal road, enjoying the beautiful scenery. Maine was just as gorgeous as Florida, but in a different way. It felt wilder, somehow, and it was easy to imagine the landscape as it would have been before people began living there.

As they neared their house, she slowed. There was a truck that she didn't recognize in their driveway. When she saw the dark form move slowly around the side of the house, her pulse quickened. Something was definitely wrong. Gripping the wheel tightly, she glanced at her grandmother. Nonna was looking out the side window, and hadn't noticed anything yet.

"Can you get my cellphone out of my purse?" she asked her grandmother as she sped up.

"Sure, dear," Nonna said, reaching down to the bag on the floor.

Ellie pressed on the gas, and sped toward the house, hoping to catch the intruder unawares. She saw the person reach up and try one of the windows on the side of the house. Thank goodness she kept them locked. Many people in the small town didn't bother locking their doors and windows, something that Ellie had never understood.

A second later, the intruder looked over his shoulder. He must have seen them coming, because he began to hurry back toward the truck. He managed to get it started and was pulling out of the driveway by the time Ellie was close enough to see the license plate. She saw only the first couple of letters before he was too far away. For a moment, she was tempted to follow him, but knew that it was a bad idea. Her last car chase had ended with her wrecking her own vehicle, and she wasn't eager to repeat the experience.

"What the world was that about?" her grandmother asked.

"I don't know," Ellie said, frowning. "Let's go in. I'm going to call Russell."

She took the call to her room, not wanting to frighten her grandmother. By the time she had Russell on the phone, she was beginning to doubt what they had seen. Had someone really been trying to break into the house? It seemed almost unbelievable—it was broad daylight, after all—but she simply didn't have any other explanation for what had happened. She had seen the person try to get inside the window for goodness sake.

"Ellie, I want you to be careful," he said once she had related the story to him. "You're the one that found Samantha's body. It's possible that her killer might be after you for some reason."

"How would anyone know that I found the body?" Ellie said. "My name wasn't in the paper, and I certainly haven't been going around telling the town. Rose is the only person I talked to about it."

"That's a good point." He fell silent, and she imagined him frowning at his desk. "Has your grandmother said anything to anybody?"

"Of course not… Well, she did tell her swimming class about Marlowe's new phrase."

"I'll look for any connections our victim might have had to the people in that class. Ellie, please be careful. We know this person is willing to kill, so don't take any chances, all right?"

"I won't," she told him. "I promise."

CHAPTER NINE

"I'm not going in to work today."

"What? Why not?"

"What if the man that tried to break in comes back?" Ellie asked. "How can I leave you alone here without worrying about you constantly?"

"I can take care of myself," Nonna said. "I can call the police just as well as you can. Ellie, what are you going to do? You can't just never leave the house again."

"Nonna—"

"Dear, I am an adult. I can take care of myself. I know you're trying to protect me, and I do appreciate that, but you can't stay here all day, every day. What are you going to do tomorrow? And the day after?"

"Fine," Ellie said, sighing. "I'll go to work, but I'm going to keep my phone on me all day. If someone even drives past the house too slowly, I want you to call Russell, and then call me. Keep all the doors and windows locked. Don't even put Bunny out while I'm gone. I'll let her out right before I go, and remember, I'll be back early to pick her up for her vet appointment. Keep yourself safe, okay?"

"Okay, okay," Nonna said. "Go to work, dear. Have a good day, and don't worry about me."

"You know I'm going to," the younger woman said. She hugged her grandmother. "And Nonna, if someone does show up, don't do anything rash, okay? Everything in this house is replaceable. You aren't."

"That's very sweet of you, dear. I'll be careful, I promise. I may be old, but I'm not ready to go yet."

When Ellie left the house short while later, she made a quick call to Russell to let him know that her grandmother would be home all day. She was relieved when he promised he would keep an eye out for a call from her, and that he would be ready to drive over at a moment's notice.

She just wished that she had been a little bit quicker, and had managed to see the man's entire license plate. She was glad that he hadn't managed to break in before she got home, but it also meant that whatever he was after, he still hadn't gotten it.

Ellie normally enjoyed her time at work, but today, she couldn't shake the feeling of anxiety. She kept checking her phone, even though she knew that she would have heard if it went off. It was going to be a long day, but she knew her grandmother was right. She couldn't spend the rest of her life at home. She would just have to trust that things would turn out all right.

The pizza of the week was a white cheese and rosemary pizza. It had fresh rosemary mixed into the crust, and diced garlic under the gooey cheese. It was a recipe that the newest employee, Pete, had come up with. She was continually impressed with all her employees' creativity, and their willingness to participate in every facet of the pizzeria, not just working shifts and clocking out. When she opened the second pizzeria, she hoped that she would be just as lucky with the employees that they would hire in Florida.

It was an unusually busy afternoon. The first customers walked in not long after she unlocked the doors, and she ran back and forth from the kitchen steadily after that. It didn't help that the rosemary pizza took longer to make, since it had a special crust, and it was the most popular pizza by far. She was so busy trying to get everyone's orders out on time that she almost didn't recognize the young man whose order she was taking. She thought that he looked somewhat familiar, but it took her a moment to place him. When she caught the whiff of chlorine from his hair, she realized that he was her grandmother's swim instructor.

"Can I have a personal-size rosemary pizza and a bottle of soda?" he asked. "That will be for here."

"Sure thing. Cash or card?" she asked.

"Card," he said, reaching into his wallet.

She was secretly pleased. She had been hoping to get his name, but didn't know how to ask without raising suspicion. She had only ever seen him from a distance before. According to her grandmother, the instructor had left part way through the class. That would have given him plenty of time to drive to the Pacelli house when they were out at lunch and try to break in. She didn't know why he would be involved in the murder, but it seemed like too much of a coincidence to ignore.

She took his card and memorized the name on the front. Brent Swan. She knew that she might just be grasping at straws, but at least she would have something new to share with Russell.

While Brent was waiting for his order, Ellie heard the employee door open and shut. She passed Rose on the way back to the kitchen—she was going to take Brent's pizza out of the oven, and Rose was coming out to the register to clock in. When Ellie came back out, she found Rose and the swim instructor engaged in conversation.

"Sorry," her employee said. "We were just talking about Samantha. I can go take over in the kitchen if you want."

83

"Oh, did you know her?" Ellie asked, handing the pizza over counter to him.

"Yeah. She was my ex," Brent said. "We were still pretty close, even after we broke up. It was horrible to hear about her."

"I'm so sorry," Ellie said automatically as her thoughts raced. This man, the swimming instructor who'd overheard her grandmother talking about Marlowe's new phrase, happened to be the pet sitter's ex-boyfriend—and the only real suspect that Russell had.

"It was very unexpected," Brent said. "I keep forgetting that she's gone, and when I remember, it's a shock all over again."

"I'm sure it is. She seemed like a wonderful young woman."

Ellie waited until he was settled outside on the patio with his food before going back into the kitchen to make the call to Russell. The sheriff needed to know about this, and as soon as possible. With luck, Samantha's killer would be behind bars before the day was over.

CHAPTER TEN

Ellie left Papa Pacelli's early to pick Bunny up for her vet appointment. The Kittiport Veterinary Clinic was a small building just outside of town, near the White Pine Kitchen. She had been there only once before for the dog's yearly exam. Unfortunately, they didn't see birds. The exotic animal clinic was down in Portland—an hour's drive away. She would be taking Marlowe in sometime the next week, when she had more time.

Bunny was normally excited to go everywhere, but that morning she seemed to know that she was on her way to the vet's office. Ellie sighed when the little dog refused to move out the front door. This happened every time they went to a vet. Ellie always wondered what she did to give their destination away. She had yet to figure it out.

Eventually, after a little coaxing, they were on their way. Bunny pouted on the passenger seat next to Ellie. After everything that she had been through, her owner felt bad making her go through another traumatic experience, even if it was for her own good.

"I don't know why you hate vets so much," Ellie said. "You won't even be getting any shots this time. He's just going to look you over, and send you on your way home. If you're lucky, there might even be some treats involved."

The papillon's ears perked up at the word treat. Ellie chuckled. At least the little dog still had her appetite.

There arrived a good fifteen minutes early for their appointment. Ellie sat in the waiting room with the dog on her lap. There was only one other person there—an older woman with a beautiful golden retriever. Bunny was wiggling with excitement at the sight of the other dog. Ellie wished that she knew more people in town with pets. Back in Chicago, she had set up playdates for Bunny with other people who owned little dogs. In Kittiport, however, she didn't really know anyone that she could do that with.

At least the dog seemed to have an affectionate, if peculiar relationship with Marlowe. The bird enjoyed tossing pellets out of her cage for the dog to eat. Then again, the bird also enjoyed shouting "bad dog" at the most random times, which scared poor Bunny half to death.

"Bunny?"

"That's us," Ellie said. She set the dog on the floor, and they walked toward the exam room. Bunny whined and walked slowly with her tail tucked between her legs, looking more pitiful than ever. When they got to the room, Ellie lifted her onto the cold metal table. The dog was shaking.

"It's okay, sweetie," Ellie said. To the tech, a young woman with dyed black hair and a nametag that read *Alaina,* she said "I don't know why, but she does this whenever we come to the vet's office."

"A lot of dogs are scared of us. They don't like all the strange smells here. We've seen her before, correct?"

"Yes, once. I moved here last year from Chicago. I'm sure you had her records transferred over."

"Yep, it looks like we did. Well, she's up to date on her shots. Why are you here today?"

"I don't know if you heard, but a woman was found dead a few days ago. That was my pet sitter. She passed away while watching my animals, and they were left without food and water for a few days. I just wanted to bring her in to make sure that everything is going okay. She lost a little bit of weight while she was there, and has seemed a little bit down since I got her back."

"How has she been acting differently?" the tech asked, pulling out her stethoscope and reaching for Bunny to hear her heartbeat.

"She's been a little bit clingier, and I think she's more anxious about certain things. She still loves food, so at least that hasn't changed." She waited silently while the tech listened to her dog's heartbeat, then checked her teeth, eyes, and ears.

"Well, she looks okay to me. The vet will be in shortly to give her a once over. It may be a few minutes, since he's with another client. There's a jar of treats on the counter.

Feel free to give her a few if you think that would help calm her down."

Ellie helped Bunny off the cold table and down to the floor. They sat silently for a few minutes, Ellie passing her a treat every now and then. Before too long, there was a soft knock at the door.

"Come on in," she said. The door opened and in walked an elderly man. Ellie recognized him as the same person who had examined Bunny last time. "Hi, Dr. Morgan."

"Hello, Ms. Pacelli," he said as he went over her file. "So, I hear you're the one that found our poor Samantha?"

"Yes. I'm very sorry about her."

"Me too. She was a nice girl," he said. "I was sad to hear about her passing."

"The whole thing was terrible. I feel bad for the animals too, trapped like that with no one to feed or water them."

"And poor Bunny here went through that. Let's take a look."

Ellie put Bunny back up on the table and waited while the vet looked her over. Bunny stood still, cowering as he poked and prodded her with his hands.

"Well, everything checks out. Her temperature is normal, there's a healthy color to her gums, and I don't feel any lumps or bumps. She's underweight, but I'm sure you're working on that. According to her file she was a bit overweight last time she came in."

"Yes. I've been feeding her a little extra to help get her weight back up."

"Make sure you don't overdo it," said. "She's a little dog, so every ounce makes a difference."

"Okay. I'll be sure to keep an eye on it. I'll have to tell my grandmother to quit feeding extra once she's back up to normal."

He chuckled. "Ann has quite a big heart, doesn't she?"

"Yes, she does." She had forgotten that the vet knew her grandmother. It really was a small town.

"Well, you're good to go. Don't worry about stopping at the front desk on the way out. I made sure to tell them that this appointment is on the house."

"Oh, really?" Ellie said. "Thank you, but why?"

"Well, I have a date with your grandmother tonight." He smiled. "A woman like that, I want to make sure I'm on her good side."

So, this was her grandmother's mysterious date. No wonder she hadn't recognized the name. She knew the vet only as Dr. Morgan, and hadn't had a clue that his first name was George. She fought back a smile as she carried the dog out. Her grandmother, dating. What was the world coming to?

CHAPTER ELEVEN

Back at home, Ellie let Bunny get settled in before she approached her grandmother. "Well, it was a pleasant vet visit," she said casually. "Dr. Morgan let us go without charging us."

"Oh, did he?" the older woman said.

"Yep."

Her grandmother sighed. "He told you about our date, didn't he?" she asked.

"He sure did. Why didn't you tell me you were going to go on a date with the town's veterinarian? I think that's wonderful."

No, it's embarrassing," her grandmother said. "I haven't gone on a date since your grandfather passed away. This is nothing serious. I don't want you getting your hopes up.

94

It's just dinner. I only said yes because I would have felt bad saying no. His wife passed away the year before Arthur did."

"I think it's sweet that you're going to dinner with him. He seems like a nice man."

"I guess it's part of my new plan to experience life more," her grandmother said. "The trip to Florida made me realize that I still have lots of options."

"That's a good thing," Ellie said. "If you want any help getting ready for your date, just let me know. I want everything to go perfectly for you."

At a quarter past four, her grandmother came into the living room where Ellie was reading. "All right, I give up. I need your help. I can't decide what to wear. Now, don't get all excited! This doesn't mean I'm trying to impress him—I just don't want to embarrass myself."

Ellie grinned and put her book down. "Let's go look at the options." She rose and followed the older woman back to her bedroom.

"Well, it's between these three," her grandmother said, gesturing to the outfits which she had laid out on the bed. There was a mint green pantsuit, which the older woman had purchased in Florida, a white summer dress with a floral pattern, and a more somber dusty pink evening dress. "We're eating at the White Pine Kitchen. I'm not sure how formally I should dress. I know that times are changing. What do you think would be best?"

Ellie stepped back and got a good look at the outfits. "I think the one with the floral print is best," she said. "It's very summery, and it's got a classic cut. It won't make you look underdressed or overdressed. Plus, it's mostly white, so it will show off the tan you got in Florida well."

"That's a good point. And I've got these little flats to wear with it. Thanks, Ellie, I'll go with this one."

After her grandmother put on the floral dress, she sat down at her vanity and Ellie helped her with her hair and her makeup. It was nice to see her grandmother so excited about something, even though she knew the older woman would never admit it. She was glad that she was willing to go on dates, even if it was just a casual dinner with a man that she had known for years. She doubted that her grandmother would start another committed relationship, but it would be wonderful for her to have someone to go out with every now and then for dinner.

Nonna's date was right on time. Ellie was waiting with her at the front door when he pulled into the driveway. She gave her grandmother a quick hug and wished her a happy evening, then watched anxiously as she walked down the steps of the front stoop. The porch lit her way down the little stone pathway to the driveway. Dr. Morgan got out and opened the passenger side door for her. Ellie saw her grandmother wave before the dome light shut off. Then they were gone, and she went back inside, feeling more emotional than she had expected. Was this how her mother had felt when Ellie had gone on her first date?

She wandered back into the kitchen, wondering if there were any decent leftovers in the fridge. She had been so focused on her grandmother's date that she hadn't considered what she was going to do for dinner. *Maybe Russell is free*, she thought. She picked up her phone from the counter where it was charging and saw that she had a missed call from Rose. Wondering what the young woman could need so late in the evening, she hit the redial button.

"Thank goodness you called back, Ms. P," her employee said. "I tried calling the sheriff on the number he gave me, but he isn't answering. I thought he might be with you, so that's why I called."

"What's going on, Rose?" Ellie asked.

"Okay, well I was online and I saw this post from Brent's current girlfriend, Alaina," the young woman said. "It's horrible. She said that she was glad that Samantha died, and that she had gotten what she deserved. She deleted it a little bit later, but I got a screenshot of it. I was just thinking… maybe she had something to do with it? I mean, she would totally have had motive. Brent and Samantha were still super good friends. Maybe she got jealous. Or maybe they got into some sort of fight at work or something."

"What do you mean?"

"Alaina works at the same vet clinic that Samantha used to," Rose said. "She's the vet's granddaughter."

CHAPTER TWELVE

Russell looked at the young man sitting across the table from him. Brent Swan just did not look like a murderer. His gut was telling him that this was all wrong, but he had the guy in—he might as well question him. Besides, he didn't trust his gut completely, not anymore.

"So, you're telling me that you have no alibi for the day of Samantha's death?" he said.

"I was at home all evening. I was sick. I don't know what else to tell you." The young man was pale, and he was starting to look worried. They had already gone over this same question a few times. Sometimes suspects would change their stories, but not Brent.

"How would you describe your relationship with Samantha?"

"It was good," he said, perking up as if glad he had finally been asked something that he could actually answer. "We stayed friends, even after we broke up. We'd gone to high school together, and we dated on and off for a few years."

"What was the cause of your most recent breakup?" the sheriff asked.

"She wanted to focus more on work and school," he said. "She was paying her way through college with the money from the veterinary clinic and from the pet-sitting gig she had on the side. She said that she wanted to work all summer, and wouldn't have time for a boyfriend. I told her that was fine. Our relationship was pretty casual, and I already had my eye on someone else anyway."

"Did the two of you have any major arguments in the weeks preceding her death?"

"No, man, I'm telling you, we got along fine. I don't think we ever had any major arguments at all."

Russell sighed and ran his hands through his hair. This guy really wasn't panning out as a suspect. He had no motive, for one, there was absolutely no physical evidence tying him to the crime for another. He had half hoped that the kid might just come out and confess it under pressure, but either he was innocent, or he was a great liar.

"Did you go over to Samantha's house for drinks at all that day?"

"No. I don't drink at all, man. My dad, he had a problem with drinking. It killed him. I never wanted to chance it."

This really wasn't going anywhere. The kid didn't do it. Now both his gut and his mind were screaming that at him, and he trusted his mind. What he was doing here was wasting his time. He was almost relieved when the knock at the door came.

"C'mon in," he grunted. It was Ms. Lafferre, the department's secretary. She jerked her head, indicating that she wanted to speak with him. He rose, told the boy to wait, and followed her.

"What is it?"

"Someone's on the phone for you. She said that she has some information about the case you're working on. I wouldn't normally interrupt an interview, but she said that Ms. Pacelli told her to call, and I know that you said her calls have priority."

"Yes, thank you. Forward the call my office, then go and offer that young man in there a cup of water. I'm not sure how long this will take."

He strode down the hall and let himself into his office. Ellie had asked someone to call him? He was consumed by worry. Why wouldn't she just call him herself? He loved the woman, but her propensity for finding trouble didn't make his life any easier. He didn't think that he had ever worried over someone as much as he worried over her. He had finally fallen for someone for the first time since his wife's death, and she was probably the most danger-prone woman in town.

The phone on his desk beeped. He grabbed at it. "Hello? This is Sheriff Ward."

"This is Rose, we spoke before," she said. "I work at the pizzeria for Ms. P. Anyway, she said I should try calling the main line at the sheriff's department. I'm friends online with this girl who's dating Samantha's ex, and she posted something on social media about the poor girl who died, and I thought it sounded a bit suspicious so I took a screenshot before she deleted it. I don't know if it's important or not. Should I send it to you?"

It took Russell a moment to sort through the girl's rambling. "You did the right thing. There should be an email address on the card I gave you. Can you attach the screenshots and send them to me? I'll see what I can do."

"Okay. Oh, and one more thing. This girl is the veterinarian's granddaughter. I don't know why that's important, but Ellie seemed kind of worried when I told her. She said something about her grandmother and hung up in a hurry. I just thought you might want to know."

"Something about her grandmother?" Russell said.

"Yeah. I didn't catch it. She hung up too quickly."

"Thanks, Rose. Send me those photos as soon as you get off the phone, okay?"

He hung up. Russell stared at his phone, trying to fight down the growing feeling of unease. How was everything connected? What did the veterinarian's granddaughter have to do with Ann Pacelli? He pulled his cellphone out of his pocket, hoping to see a message from Ellie, but the only missed call was the one from Rose. He dialed his girlfriend's number, but was unsurprised when the line rang through to voicemail. Ellie was almost as bad about keeping her phone on silent as he was.

"Ellie, please call when you get a chance," he said. He made sure that the ringer's volume was up, then turned on his computer to wait for the girl's email. Nothing seem to have gone according to plan since Ellie had gotten home. He had been all set up to propose to her that evening, when he had gotten the call about Samantha. He knew that he should have done it at the restaurant during their date, but he had kept putting it off until somehow, he was paying for the bill and they were leaving with the ring still in his pocket. He didn't know how he could face down a murder at gunpoint, but was terrified by the thought of getting down on one knee and asking Ellie to marry him. What if she said no? He kept telling himself that he was waiting for the perfect moment, but the truth was, he was being a coward.

The computer dinged. He had received an email. He opened it up and waited as the files loaded. At long last, he could read the post by Alaina Morgan, the post that had freaked Rose out so much that she had called him.

I know this is an unpopular opinion, but Samantha got what she deserved. She was sticking her nose where it didn't belong, and she got what was coming to her. Whoever killed her doesn't deserve jail time. They deserve an award.

It was time to let Brent go. The young man's new girlfriend had just become their lead suspect.

PATTI BENNING

CHAPTER THIRTEEN

Ellie drove toward the White Pine Kitchen, trying to sort through the thoughts dancing in her head. Was Alaina the killer? If so, did that mean Nonna was in danger? If the vet had mentioned to his granddaughter that Marlowe had begun saying something from the day of the murder, then Alaina might begin to worry. The two family members worked together at a vet clinic, and they must both love animals. She would be surprised if the elderly man hadn't shared the story of his date's crazy macaw screaming out a woman's last words. If Alaina's online post didn't mark her as the killer, then Ellie didn't know what would. No normal person would be glad that someone had been murdered, and no sane person would post it online.

She didn't know what she was going to do when she got to the restaurant. She didn't want to wreck her grandmother's date, but she didn't want to risk Alaina crashing it either.

She pulled into the parking lot and jumped out of her vehicle, not even bothering to take the time to lock it. She pushed through the doors and paused, ignoring the hostess who was speaking to her. It wasn't until she recognized her grandmother's bright white hair at a table far across the room that she gave a sigh of relief and relaxed. She and George Morgan were alone at their little table, with no sign of his dark-haired granddaughter anywhere nearby.

Ellie turned to the waitress. "It will just be me," she said. "Can I get one of the booths over there?" She pointed to the opposite side of the restaurant from her grandmother.

The hostess led her over to a booth that was positioned perfectly for Ellie's needs—she could see the door, and if she stretched, she could see her grandmother's table. She sat down, ordered salad and a glass of wine, and waited. If her grandmother left with anyone other than the veterinarian, she would see it. She was probably just paranoid after what happened in Florida, but she wasn't going to let her grandmother be kidnapped again.

She took out her phone to check her email and realized that she had missed a call from Russell. She listened to his message, which wasn't very informative, then called him back.

"Hello?"

"It's me. I'm returning your call. What's up?"

"Ellie, I'm glad you're all right. I was just talking to Rose. She mentioned your conversation, and that you said you were worried about your grandmother and hung up suddenly. It made me worried. What's going on?"

"Nonna is on a date with Dr. Morgan, Alaina's grandfather. I know I was probably just overreacting, but I thought about how easy it would be for Alaina to wiggle her way in and do something to Nonna. After what happened in Florida, I'm being extra careful I guess. It just seemed like an odd coincidence to me."

"Where are you now?"

"I'm at the White Pine Kitchen. I just had some wine and I'm watching the door. I'll see if Alaina comes in."

"Okay. Let me know if she does. I'm going to see if I can track her down and bring her in for questioning. Between her dating the victim's ex, and her and Samantha having issues at work, there's definitely a motive there."

"I agree," Ellie said. "I'm going to keep sitting here until my grandmother leaves. I guess it's better to be safe than sorry, especially since you think that something is up too."

"Okay," Russell said. "Keep your phone on, okay? I want to be able to get through to you if I need to call you."

"Of course. You be careful too."

"I always am."

She hung up and made sure that her phone had plenty of charge, then she settled back with her wine and tried to think things through while she waited. Samantha had worked at the vet clinic until just a few weeks ago. Alaina had been her coworker, and perhaps competition—Brent had obviously been interested in both of them. She was willing to bet that the two women hadn't gotten along. Had Alaina had something to do with Samantha losing her job? There was no telling what sort of drama had gone on between the two women, either work or boy related. Brent, it seemed, had been caught in the middle of all of this. If Russell was focusing his sights on Alaina, then Ellie would too. She trusted his judgment. After all, he had never been wrong about something like this before, had he?

PATTI BENNING

CHAPTER FOURTEEN

An hour and a half, an appetizer, and two glasses of wine later, Ellie saw her grandmother and Dr. Morgan leave the White Pine Kitchen together. She rose from her seat and followed them to the door, watching the parking lot long enough to be sure that they were the only two people to get into the vehicle. There was no sign of the dark-haired vet tech anywhere. She was relieved. Hopefully by now Russell had found the woman and had her at the sheriff's department for questioning.

She drove slowly on the way home, not wanting to pull into the driveway just as her grandmother was getting home. She would give them their privacy. The long way home would take a good fifteen extra minutes, and it would be scenic, even at night. The stars outside of town were gorgeous, especially on a clear summer night like this.

When she eventually made her way to the house, she was surprised to see that the vet's vehicle was still in the driveway when she pulled up, with no one in it. She wondered if her grandmother had invited him over for dessert. She had made some chocolate cookies earlier that she hadn't let Ellie touch.

Ellie let herself into the house. "Nonna?" she called. It was oddly quiet in the house, and she couldn't hear their voices anywhere.

When there was no answer, she continued on inside. She saw that Marlow's food dish had been spilled in her cage, and the bird was clinging upside down to the top of it. She was breathing heavily and—to Ellie's surprise—the cage door was unlatched. Ellie was surprised that Bunny wasn't there. Normally she would be gorging herself on the spilled food.

"Bunny?" she called. "Nonna? Anyone? What's going on?"

She was beginning to worry now. She walked into the kitchen, and was shocked to see the back door was wide open. She went outside, calling for her dog. Bunny was nowhere to be found, and there was also no sign of Nonna. No sign, other than a few chocolate chip cookies scattered in the yard.

Ellie stared at the mess, then glanced back toward the house. She had no idea what could have happened. Where was everyone? Suddenly she heard a high-pitched yap coming from the trees.

"Bunny?" she called out, louder this time, as she began to jog toward the forest. Chances were the little dog was with her grandmother, though why either of them would be in the forest was beyond her. She felt a sharp twinge of worry as she heard the barking again. Bunny would be easy prey for any number of predatory animals that lived in the forest, and her grandmother wouldn't be much better off.

Maybe they just went on a walk together, she thought. *They could have forgotten to latch the back door, and Marlowe might have opened her own cage… but the cookies, I have no explanation for those.*

116

She hurried toward the forest, breaking into an all-out run when she heard Bunny begin to bark again. She pushed her way through the bushes that bordered the yard and began to shout for her grandmother.

"Nonna? Bunny? Where are you?"

The little dog's barking was getting closer. She followed the sound, and was relieved when she saw the white flash of the dog's fur in between the trees. She hurried forward, so focused on the dog that she almost didn't see what she was barking at. She froze when she saw Dr. Morgan standing in front of her. He was holding a wooden cane up as if he had been about to strike at the dog, and was staring at her with a stunned expression on his face.

"What are you doing here?" he asked roughly.

"I could ask you the same thing," Ellie said, clutching the dog to her chest. "What are you doing out here? What happened in the house? Where is my grandmother?"

"I came out here to look at her," the man said, lowering his cane. "The dog followed me."

"Why would Nonna be out here?" Ellie asked.

"I don't know. The crazy old bat invited me in for cookies, then ran off into the forest for no reason at all."

"You have no right to talk to her about her like that," Ellie said. She frowned at the man, then looked around. Why would her grandmother do that? She supposed it was possible that the man wasn't lying, but what would cause the older woman to act like that? Her grandmother might be in her eighties, but her mind was usually very clear.

"Nonna?" she shouted. "If you're here, follow my voice."

"Enough of that," the man said.

"Aren't you looking for her too?"

"I was—"

He was cut off by a shout from the opposite direction. "Ellie?"

Ellie felt a rush of relief. She recognized her grandmother's voice.

"I'm here, Nonna. Head this way."

"Ellie, you get away from that man. He's dangerous."

Ellie spun around, but it was too late. Dr. Morgan was already swinging his cane at her. It struck her across the temple, hard enough to make her stumble backward. She might have kept to her feet if her shoe hadn't caught on a fallen branch, but she landed heavily on her rear. As she was struggling to catch her breath, Bunny struggled out of her arms and ran straight toward the vet, barking fiercely. Ellie pressed her fingers to her temple and was surprised when they came away dry. She wasn't bleeding, even though it felt like he had hit her hard enough to split her skull open.

"Get off me, you little rat," she heard the vet say. She blinked, trying to focus, and saw Bunny tugging at the man's pant leg with her teeth. He raised the cane, and brought it down sharply at the little dog.

"No!" she shouted. It was too late. She heard Bunny yelp as the cane struck her. There was a sharp crack, and the little dog's body went flying away from him. Ellie stared at her still form, begging her to get up, but she didn't move.

Ellie pulled herself to her feet, feeling hot rage wash through her. The man had hurt her dog. Tears pricked her eyes. Him hitting Bunny made her even angrier than when he had hit her. She took a step toward him, not sure what she was about to do. He took half a step back and raised his cane again, when they were both distracted by the sound of snapping sticks and crunching leaves. Ellie looked up to see her grandmother hurrying toward them as quickly as she could. Her dress was torn and she was missing a shoe, but other than the large bruise on her arm, she seemed all right.

"You stay away from my granddaughter," Nonna said. She hefted a rock in her hand. "This will hurt a lot more than those cookies did. You already know I have good aim."

"Neither of you move," Dr. Morgan said. He shuffled backward and ducked down to pick up Bunny's limp form. When he touched her, the little dog stirred and whimpered. She was still alive. Ellie closed her eyes, relieved. It wasn't too late for them all to get out of this alive.

The vet reached into his pocket and pulled out a syringe. "Neither of you move. This syringe is filled with enough barbiturates to kill a dog ten times her size."

Ellie bit her lip, and reached out a hand to stop her grandmother, who had been adjusting her grip on the rock. She didn't know whether he was telling the truth or not, but she didn't want to risk it.

"Please don't hurt her," she said. "She was just protecting me."

"I won't hurt her if you do what I say. Neither of you follow me out of the woods. I don't want to hear a single twig snap while I'm still in here, understand?"

Ellie is that looked at her grandmother and nodded. Nonna frowned, but eventually managed a nod as well. The vet began to slowly back away. Ellie felt her heart pound as he disappeared into the trees with her dog. How had all of this happened?

"What's going on?" She whispered to her grandmother as the elderly man's footsteps gradually faded.

"I don't know. We had a nice date and he drove me home. I invited him in for cookies. I went to the kitchen to grab the plate, and when I came out, he had his hands in Marlowe's cage and was trying to stick a needle in her. I yelled at the top of my lungs for him to stop. I think I gave him quite the scare, because he took off. I started pelting him with cookies, then when I ran out I threw the plate too. I got a little carried away and followed him into the woods. Bunny must have followed me. He hid behind a tree and surprised me. He got in one good hit with the cane, but I managed to get away." She showed Ellie the bruise. "I was going to start circling back to the house, but then I heard you. Are you all right?"

"Yes, he hit me with his cane, but thankfully he's not as strong as a younger man might have been. I think I'll be fine." Ellie bit her lip. She hated just standing there, but she didn't want to put Bunny's life in danger by following him too soon. "Why would he want to hurt Marlowe?"

"I don't know." Her grandmother looked at the ground. "Do you think it's my fault? For telling him about

Marlowe saying, 'stop it' the other day? Maybe he thinks she knows too much."

"Even if that's the reason he did all of this, it's not your fault," Ellie said. She frowned. Things were beginning to make sense, at least a little bit. Maybe Alaina wasn't the killer after all—her grandfather was. If Samantha had found out something that would threaten his veterinary practice, maybe he had killed her to keep her quiet. And maybe he was afraid that Marlowe would say his name one of these days.

Ellie decided that they had waited long enough. "Hurry," she said. "We have to follow him. I have to find a way to stop him before he kills Marlowe."

CHAPTER FIFTEEN

Ellie and her grandmother crept slowly through the trees. The pizzeria owner was hyperaware of every sound. She didn't want to catch up to the doctor too quickly, in case he made good on his threat to kill Bunny. She didn't want to move too slowly, either. If she didn't come up with a plan before he got to the house, then he would kill Marlowe.

The bird wasn't the only one in danger. He might not be thinking straight right now, but it wouldn't take the vet long to realize that she and her grandmother couldn't be left as witnesses. He would have to kill them all. The only question was, how would he try to do it?

By the time she and Nonna reached the edge of the woods, the old veterinarian was nowhere in sight. They had been too slow—he must have reached the house already. Ellie shot a glance toward her grandmother. She was torn between running as fast as she could toward the house, and her desire to stay with the older woman to protect her.

"Go," Nonna said, reading the look in her eyes. "I'll follow as quickly as I can."

Ellie took off running across the yard. It was nearly dark now, and she could barely see where she was going, but it didn't matter. She walked through this yard every day with Bunny, and she probably could have run through it with her eyes closed. She knew where every hole and hill was, even in the dark.

The back door was still open when she reached it. She slipped inside silently, edging through the kitchen. Suddenly she heard a loud squawk, then a man cursing loudly. She tossed caution to the wind and rushed forward, bracing herself for what she might find. What she wasn't expecting was Russell holding tightly to Dr. Morgan's hands. Behind them, in the corner, Bunny was lying on her side. Marlowe, her feathers ruffled, was crouching on top of her cage with a wild look in her eyes.

"Ellie, he's the killer. I found him out about to stick a needle in your bird. Where is your grandmother? Is she okay?"

"Yes, she's fine. How did you know it was him? You got here just in time."

"I was coming over to… for something else. I knew something was wrong when I saw his truck in the driveway. Alaina told me everything. Liam and Bethany are out looking for him as we speak." The last sentence was directed toward Dr. Morgan. Russell tightened his grip on the old veterinarian's wrists and pulled a pair of handcuffs out of his pocket with his other hand. Ellie heard the metallic sound of them being secured firmly around the man's wrists. "He was stealing drugs from the clinic and selling them. Samantha found out and was going to turn him in, so he fired her. It didn't take him long to realize what a mistake he had made." Russell glared at the doctor and continued, "I'm guessing the drinks were your way of trying to make it harder for her to defend herself. It was messy, but it worked in the end. You managed to shove her into the door, where she hit her head and died."

The veterinarian shook his head. "I never meant to kill her like that. It was supposed to be a clean death. I'm not a barbarian."

"You didn't mean to shove her so hard, did you?" Ellie asked, looking from his face to the needle on the floor. "You were going to inject her with drugs, just like you were trying to do with Marlowe."

"It was supposed to be a clean death," Dr. Morgan said. "But she saw me with a needle in my hand and she panicked. I had to hit her with my cane, and she tripped and fell against the door. It's not how I wanted to do it. If I had been able to stick with my plan, you never would have been able to tell it was murder. A young woman who lost her job and her boyfriend in the same month, found dead with a needle in her arm… you would have called it a suicide."

"You have the right to remain silent," Russell said, turning Dr. Morgan toward the door. "But go ahead and keep talking. I'm going to love using all of this against you in court."

Russell phoned his deputy, and Liam arrived to take the old veterinarian down to the sheriff's department, where he would spend the night in a holding cell before beginning the long journey to prison. Once he was gone and Ellie was satisfied that Nonna and Marlowe were both okay, she picked up Bunny and gently carried the little dog to the car, where she sat holding her in the passenger seat while Russell drove them to the emergency vet the next town over.

There, they confirmed Ellie's fear. The little dog had a broken leg. Ellie knew that Bunny had gotten lucky; if the cane had hit her any other way, it could have easily broken her spine. She felt a sharp surge of hatred toward the veterinarian. He was supposed to help animals, not hurt them. Bunny had been no threat to him—she weighed barely seven pounds. He had struck at her purely out of malice.

She wanted to stay and wait while Bunny was in surgery, but the vet staff convinced her to go home and return in the morning to pick up the dog. She felt terrible walking away, but she knew that they were right; her waiting there all night would only make her exhausted the next day. She had to trust that Bunny was in good hands—better hands than the ones that had hurt her.

By the time that she and Russell got back to the house, the lights were all off and she knew that her grandmother would already be asleep. Russell walked her up to the front door, where they paused.

"You never told me, what were you doing here?" she asked.

Russell hesitated. "Ellie, I know that this may not be the best time for this. But there's something I've been wanting to ask you for a long time, and if I don't do it now, I may never have the courage to do it." He reached into his pocket and slowly got down on one knee. As he did so, he pulled out a black ring box and opened it, holding it up to her. "Will you marry me?"

Ellie was stunned into silence. It took her a few seconds to find her voice again. "Yes," she whispered. "Yes, I will."

Russell slid the ring onto her finger, then rose to his feet. He pulled her close to him, wrapped his arms around her, and lowered his lips to hers for a lingering kiss.

77281342R00074

Made in the USA
Columbia, SC
30 September 2019